THIS WALKER BOOK BELONGS TO:

_____

_____

_____

_____

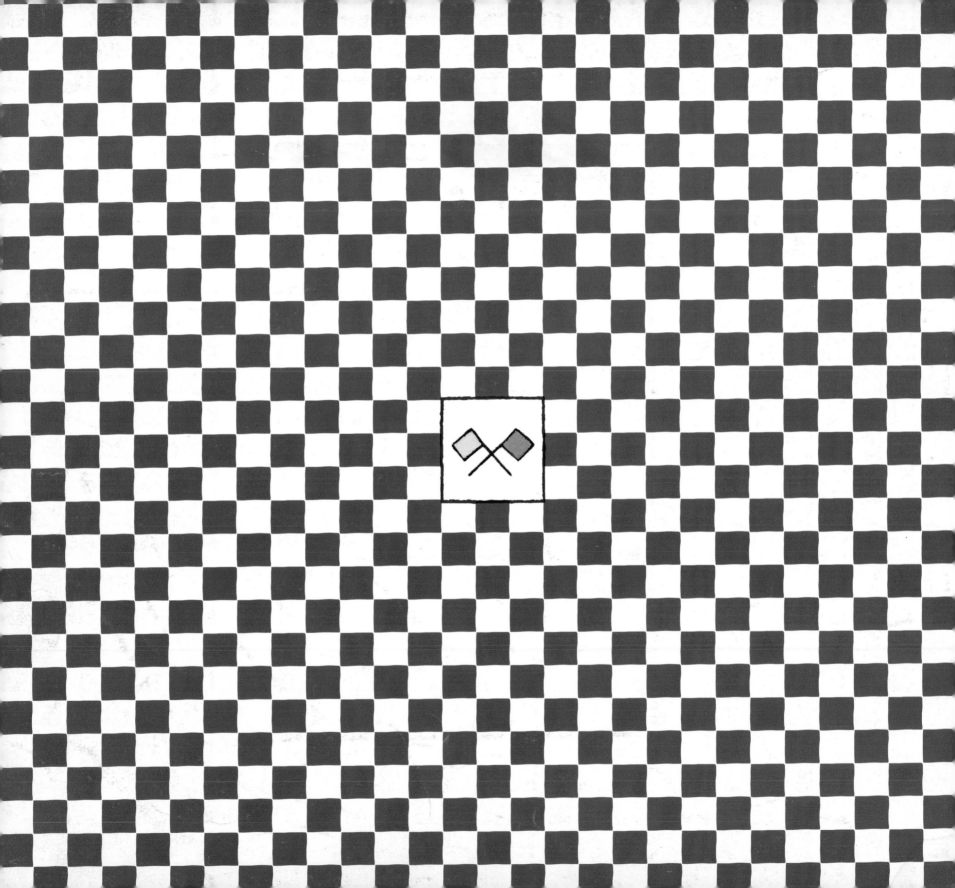

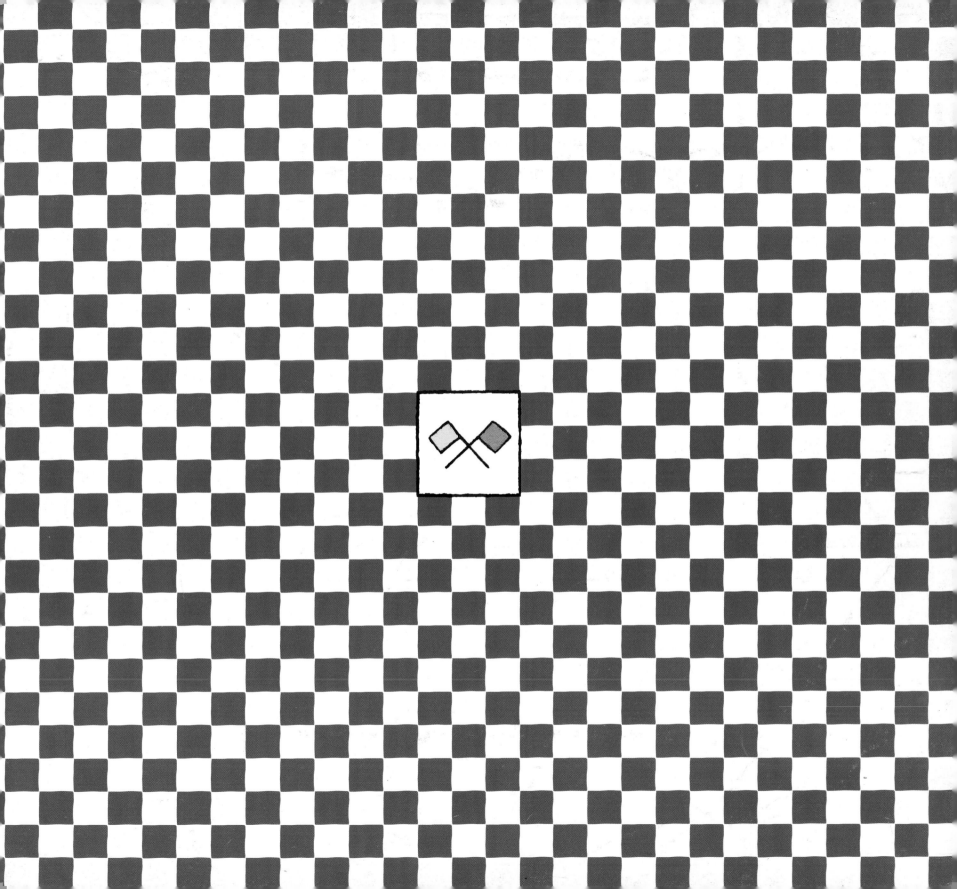

For Great Dividers everywhere
D. D.

To my family
and Dixie and Grover
T. M.

First published 2000 by Walker Books Ltd
87 Vauxhall Walk, London SE11 5HJ

This edition published 2001

2 4 6 8 10 9 7 5 3 1

Text © 2000 Dayle Ann Dodds
Illustrations © 2000 Tracy Mitchell

This book has been typeset in Handwriter.

Printed in Hong Kong

British Library Cataloguing in Publication Data
A catalogue record for this book is
available from the British Library.

ISBN 0-7445-7858-2

The Great Divide

A mathematical marathon

Written by
Dayle Ann Dodds

Illustrated by
Tracy Mitchell

WALKER BOOKS
AND SUBSIDIARIES
LONDON · BOSTON · SYDNEY

"BANG!" GOES THE GUN.
THE RACE IS ON.

A CLOUD OF DUST.
THEY'RE HERE –
THEY'RE GONE...

Pushing and pedalling side by side,

eighty begin The Great Divide.

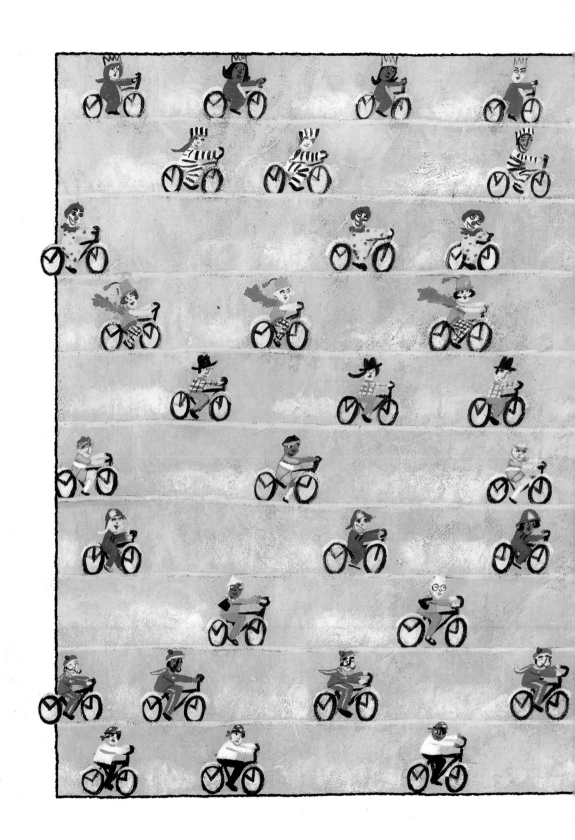

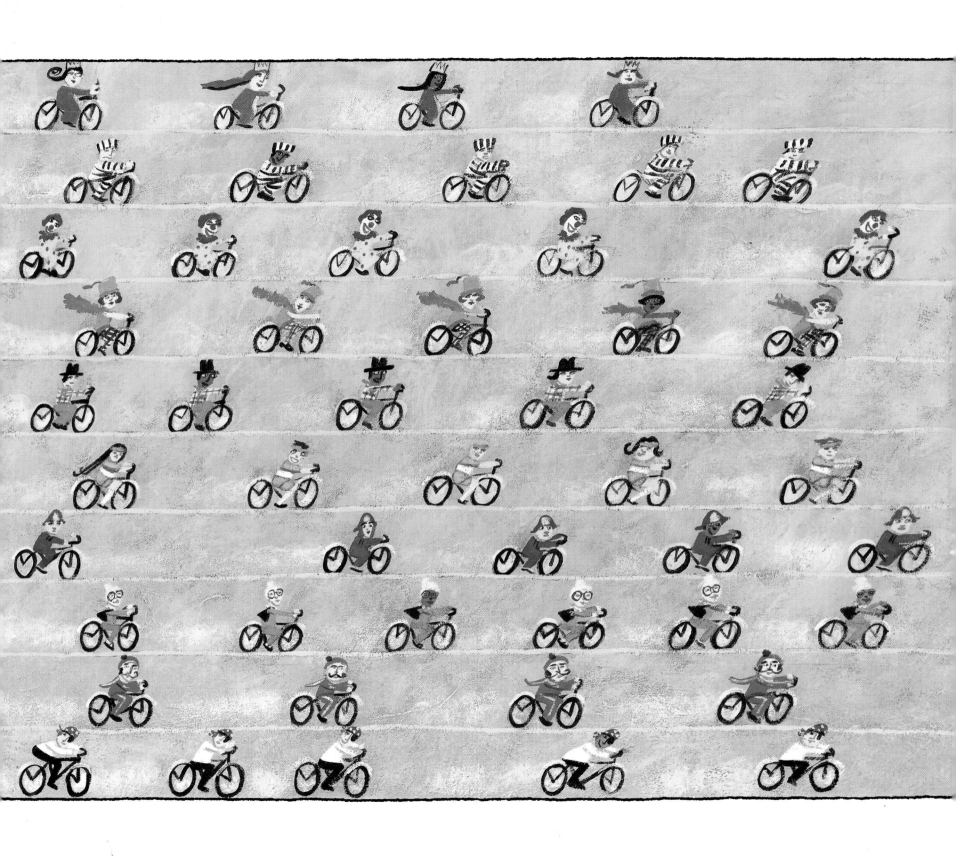

Just up ahead, just beyond sight,
one path leads left,
one path leads right.

Split by a canyon so deep
and so wide, the
riders must
part at
The
Great
D
i
v
i
d
e

Half blunder left,
where their tyres go
pop!

Half hurtle right,
never to stop.

On with the race.
Head for a boat!

40

Forty racers
now have to float!

What's up ahead?
A loud, roaring sound!
Whooshing whirlpools
spin all around.

Half are swept up
in a dizzying whirl.
Half battle on through
foam and swirl.

Out of the river,
on to dry land,

twenty racers
take to the sand.

One path turns east.
One path turns west.
Split by a mountain,
which choice is best?

Half stampede west
to a muddy disgrace.
Half gallop east
at a thunderous pace.

In hot-air balloons
floating up high,

10

ten racers
now sail through
the sky!

Half blow north
right into a storm.
Half breeze south,
safe and warm.

5

Five press on,
pushing danger aside,
determined to win
The Great Divide.

Into the city,
down the main street,
they're racing on foot—
they're in a dead heat.

One runner stops
with a stone in her shoe.

Four are now left,
split two and two.

Pedalling bicycles –
one to each pair –
they zoom on ahead
as fast as they dare.

So fast, in fact, they
can't find the brake.
With a crash
and a splash
they fall in the lake!

FINISH

A hush fills the crowd.
They look far.
They look near.
Are there no racers left?
Have they no one to cheer?

LINE!

Are there zero left over?
Are there nought?
Are there none?
Not one? Not any?
Is the race done?

Wait!

Up in the sky -
what could it be?
Roaring!
Soaring!
Who do they see?

With a wave
of her hand,
with a dip
and a glide,

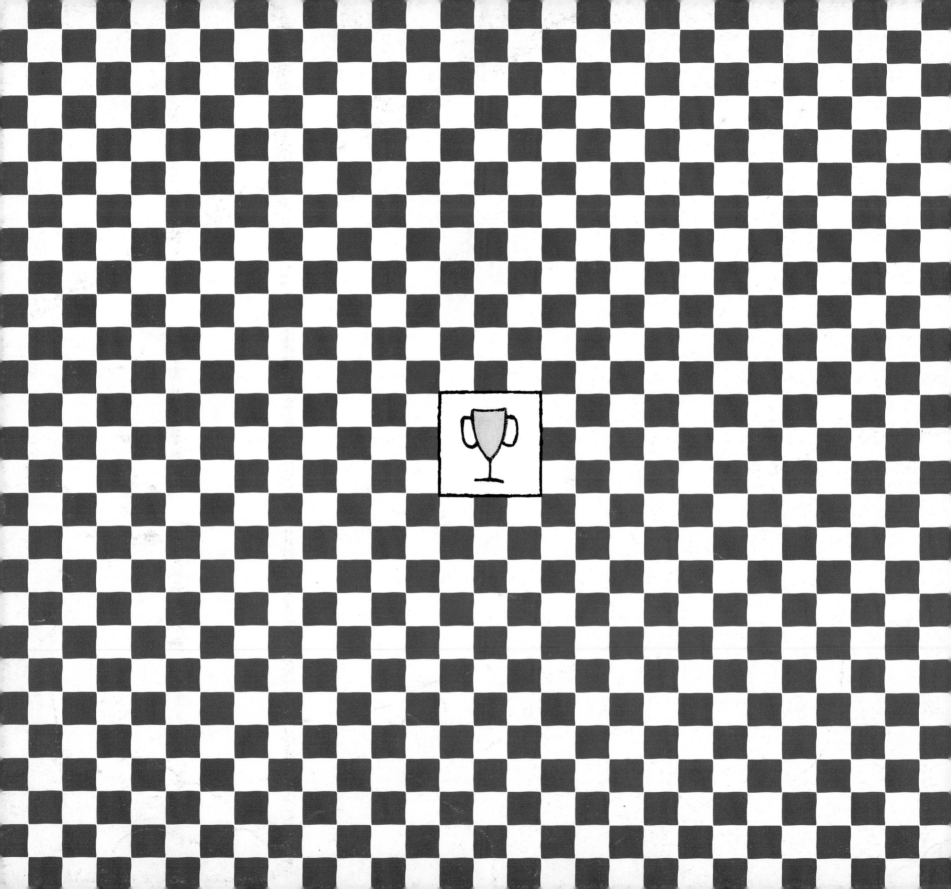

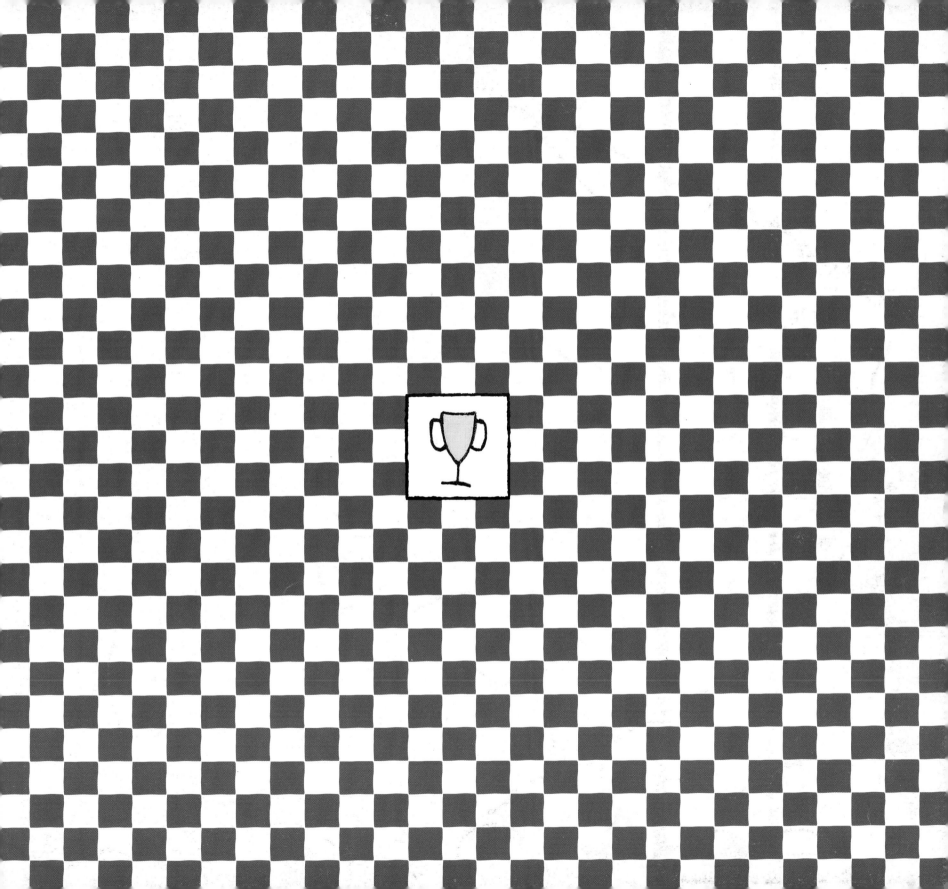

DAYLE ANN DODDS drew from a childhood memory when she decided to write **The Great Divide**. "My family took a trip to the Grand Canyon in Arizona," she says. "I was amazed at how deep and how wide it was! I wondered, how could you ever get from one side to the other?"

Dayle Ann Dodds is a former teacher. She is the author of over fifteen books for children, including *The Shape of Things* and *Sing, Sophie!* She often writes in rhyme because "it's natural to children's ears. Rhythm, rhyme and pattern," she says "help young people remember small revelations in entertaining stories." Dayle lives in Palo Alto, California, USA.

TRACEY MITCHELL says of **The Great Divide**, "I think that teaching maths using not just numbers, but words and pictures as well, can make it a lot more stimulating for children. Dividing the racers into specific groups such as dancers, sailors, prisoners etc. helps to make the division fun."

Tracey Mitchell was born in Boston but grew up in New Orleans, a city whose influence is evident in her art style. She received a degree in Illustration from the Art Institute of Boston, and now works as a freelance illustrator. *The Great Divide* is her first picture book. Tracey lives in Somerville, Massachusetts, USA.

Some more maths-related Walker picture books

ISBN 0-7445-7219-3 (pb)

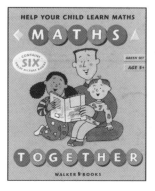

ISBN 0-7445-7220-7 (pb)

ISBN 0-7445-4754-7 (pb)

ISBN 0-7445-4368-1 (pb)